ALL YOU NEED IS NINE

Grandpa Walt showed Walter an old, yellowed piece of newspaper. It read:

THE NORTH DAKOTA NINE WIN AGAIN

"My old team in the minors," said Grandpa Walt. "In those days a lot of guys came to the league with their own teams. As long as you had nine players and a coach they had to let you in."

"I've never heard of anyone who joined the league with their own team," Walter said quietly.

His grandfather shrugged. "No law against it. You just need nine."

On the way home Grandpa Walt's words went through Walter's head. *You just need nine. I'm one*, thought Walter. *That leaves eight.*

And then Walter had a great idea. "Know where I can find a good coach?" he said with a smile.

"You're looking at him," Grandpa Walt said. "Official coach *and* driver."

And that's how the Never Sink Nine began.

Bantam Skylark Books you will enjoy
Ask your bookseller for the books you have
missed

THE NEVER SINK NINE

Walter's Lucky Socks

BY GIBBS DAVIS

Illustrated by
George Ulrich

A BANTAM SKYLARK BOOK©
NEW YORK • TORONTO • LONDON • SYDNEY • AUCKLAND

RL 2, 005–008

WALTER'S LUCKY SOCKS

A Bantam Skylark Book / April 1991

Skylark Books is a registered trademark of Bantam Books, a division of Bantam Doubleday Dell Publishing Group, Inc. Registered in U.S. Patent and Trademark Office and elsewhere.

ISBN 0-553-15865-1

Published simultaneously in the United States and Canada

Bantam Books are published by Bantam Books, a division of Bantam Double-day Dell Publishing Group, Inc. Its trademark, consisting of the words "Bantam Books" and the portrayal of a rooster, is Registered in U.S. Patent and Trademark Office and in other countries. Marca Registrada. Bantam Books, 666 Fifth Avenue, New York, New York 10103.

PRINTED IN THE UNITED STATES OF AMERICA

CWO   9 8 7 6 5 4 3 2

*For my big brother
Price Morgan, a natural
athlete and an avid
baseball fan*

CHAPTER ONE

Batboy

Mrs. Howard put the last problem on the blackboard.

9 × 7 =

Walter Dodd wrote 62 on his worksheet. It didn't look right.

Baseball tryouts for the Rockville League were this afternoon, and Walter couldn't think of anything else. He couldn't wait to play on a real team with his big brother, Danny.

He rubbed his purple socks against the leg of his chair. They were his lucky socks.

Walter looked across a row of desks at his

best friend Mike Lasky. Mike was peeling bubble gum off his face—the kind you get with a pack of baseball cards. He had the best collection in the third grade.

Walter saw Mike drop a baseball card on the floor. It was their secret signal to meet in the bathroom.

Mike was waving his hand in the air. "Can I go to the bathroom?"

Mrs. Howard didn't even look up from her desk. "Yes, Mike. And no more gum for the rest of the day, please."

Walter waited exactly one minute after Mike left the room. Then he raised his hand. "I have to go, too."

Mrs. Howard nodded.

Walter found Mike in front of the bathroom mirror. He swung an invisible bat through the air. "Swoosh!" he said.

Mike jumped up and pretended to catch the ball.

"We're going to be great at tryouts today,"

said Walter. "I hope I get to play second base on Danny's team."

Mike made a face in the mirror. "You can't play with Danny. He's ten. You're only eight."

"Eight and three-quarters," said Walter. "They'll let me. I always fill in when Danny needs an extra player."

Mike shrugged. He wet one hand and tried to smooth down his hair. A few patches were missing. When he'd gotten gum stuck in his hair Mrs. Howard had to cut it out.

"Maybe you can be an extra, too," said Walter. "I'll ask Danny."

"I can't. It's Friday." Mike pretended to play the piano on the sink.

Walter knew that meant Friday was Mike's piano lesson. He was glad his mother didn't make him take dumb lessons. It was bad enough having to take out the garbage and make his bed.

"We'd better get back," said Walter. "It's al-

most time for tryouts." He burst out the door and ran back to their classroom.

Walter kneeled on his chair. He looked at the clock. 2:53. He'd been counting the days to baseball season and now he was counting the minutes.

"All eyes on your worksheet," said Mrs. Howard. She was looking straight at Walter.

Walter sat down in his chair and looked at his problem again.

$9 \times 7 =$

Walter wrote 63. He knew that was the correct answer. He looked at the girl in front of him. Melissa Nichols had finished all her math problems and was drawing horses.

Show off, thought Walter. He inched forward. Just as he reached out to pull her long red braid, his foot hit her backpack. Something inside rattled. Walter knew what it was.

Plastic horses. Lots of them.

Melissa turned around fast. "You'd better not have hurt Misty." Melissa pulled a gray spotted horse out of her backpack. She checked it over carefully.

"Ooooooooohhhh, I'm scared." Walter pretended to shake. He crossed his eyes and pushed up his nose. It was his best gross-out face, but she wasn't even looking.

Melissa was a pain. She was loud and bossy, but she was the best pitcher in the class. She was a pretty good hitter, too. Walter was better in the field. Nothing got by his mitt.

Walter reached into his backpack and pulled out his new mitt. He punched it. The soft leather felt great under his fist. It had broken in perfectly.

"Time's up, class," said Mrs. Howard.

Walter slung his backpack over one shoulder.

"Walter, would you collect the worksheets, please?"

Walter made a face. He set down his pack. Then he hurried up and down the aisles grabbing papers. He put the pile on Mrs. Howard's desk and rushed to the door.

"Just a minute, Walter," said Mrs. Howard. "Your science project is due next Friday. How's it coming?"

"Fine." His voice came out in a squeak.

Mrs. Howard smiled. "Let me know if you need help. Your mobile of the solar system sounds quite interesting."

Walter forced a smile. He hurried back to his seat and lifted his desk top. Inside lay nine balls of different sizes.

Planets.

Walter opened his backpack and tossed the balls inside.

He'd work on his project later.

Walter was the last one out the door. He pushed his way through the crowd outside Eleanor Roosevelt Elementary.

Mike was already on his bike. He waved to Walter as he pushed off. "Later, alligator!"

"In a while, crocodile!" Walter shouted back.

Just then Walter spotted his brother Danny. He was on the other side of the playground. He ran to catch up and shoved his way into a group of fourth graders. He knew all their names. Walter felt important just being with them.

"Batboy's here," said Joey Cooke. He wore braces so everyone called him Joey "the mouth" Cooke. He dumped his bat in Walter's arms. The other boys did the same.

Walter tagged along, balancing their bats. He didn't mind. Besides, once he was on a *real* team in the Rockville League, they'd have their own batboy.

Walter stood next to his brother at the street corner across from Diamond Park. Danny was standing near Mrs. Miller, the crossing guard, waiting for the light to change.

"Can I fill in if you guys need an extra player?" Walter asked.

Danny looked embarrassed. "Why don't you play ball with kids your own age?"

"You promised," Walter reminded him.

"You promised," Joey said in a baby voice.

Walter tried to ignore Joey. He looked at

his brother. He felt like his whole life depended on Danny's answer.

"I don't know if you can," said Danny. He looked away. "Whatever the coach says, goes."

Mrs. Miller spoke to them. "Sounds like you boys are trying out for the Rockville League."

Everyone nodded, including Walter.

"Not you, squirt," said Joey, giving Walter a shove.

Before Walter had a chance to say anything the light changed. Danny and his friends grabbed their bats and crossed the street.

As soon as Walter set foot in Diamond Park he forgot all about Joey. He forgot about being too young and being the batboy and math problems and his science project. In a little while they'd be breaking up into teams. And Walter was going to be on one of them.

Walter broke into a run. He couldn't wait.

CHAPTER TWO

Tagalong Walter

Diamond Park had three baseball fields. Each one was named for a famous ballplayer— Willie Mays, Mickey Mantle, and Babe Ruth.

"Tryouts are on Willie Mays!" called Danny, running ahead with his friends. Walter followed them to the farthest diamond.

A crowd of kids gathered around the coach, Mr. Potter. Walter had never seen Mr. Potter out of the green apron he wore at his grocery store. Today Mr. Potter was wearing a sweatshirt and baseball cap. He blew the whistle hanging around his neck.

Walter squeezed up front next to Danny. He didn't want to miss one word.

"Okay, everyone!" Mr. Potter shouted so everyone could hear. "I'm Coach Potter and this afternooon we'll be holding tryouts for the Rockville League!"

All the kids around Walter began to cheer. Coach Potter grinned. He held up one hand and waited for everyone to quiet down.

"This is the time to prove yourself at bat and on the field," he said. "Now, let's play ball!"

Coach Potter picked seven kids to be out in the field. When he pointed to Walter, Walter ran straight out to second base. It was his favorite position, right in the middle of the action.

Things got off to a good start. Walter snagged two grounders and even caught a fly ball.

Hitting was a different story.

Walter jogged in and sat on the bench.

"Next," said Coach Potter when it was Walter's turn.

11

Walter took the helmet from the last batter. He stepped up to home plate.

"Name," said Coach Potter.

"Dodd."

Coach Potter went down his list. "Daniel?"

"No. Walter."

Coach Potter's forehead wrinkled. "We don't have you listed."

Walter's heart sank. Coach Potter looked at the long line of kids waiting for their turn at bat. "Go on," he said to Walter. "We'll take care of this later."

The bat felt heavy in Walter's hands. He choked up on the handle and nodded toward Danny's friend, Dave, who was the pitcher.

The first ball was a fat one. Slow and easy.

Swoooooooooosh!

Walter's bat sliced through the air. He missed the ball completely.

"Time-out," he called and laid down his bat. He grabbed hold of his lucky socks and gave them a tug. He needed all the luck he could get.

It worked.

He managed to tag the last ball for a foul.

"Next," said Coach Potter as he made a mark on his clipboard.

Walter passed the helmet to the next batter and took his place on the sidelines.

When it was Danny's turn at bat, his friends started cheering.

"Murder that sucker!" yelled Joey.

Dave threw a slow underhand ball.

Danny fired a line drive straight down center field.

"Try a few fast balls!" Coach Potter yelled to the pitcher.

Danny drove every one deep into the outfield.

"Danny the Driver!" shouted one of his pals.

Lucky duck, thought Walter. The season hadn't even begun and Danny had already earned himself a nickname.

"Okay," said Coach Potter. He stood in the

dugout studying his clipboard. After a few minutes he waved everyone in.

Everyone crowded around Coach Potter. "Listen carefully," he said. "Each player's name will be called off with their new team and sponsor."

Walter ground a fist into his mitt. This was it.

Most of Danny's friends were on the first four teams the coach called off. Walter looked over at Danny. "I'll bet we're next," he whispered. There was only one team left. He and Danny had to be on it.

Coach Potter announced the last team. "First-Class Flyers. World Travel Agency is the sponsor. David Beckman, Matthew Cole . . ."

Right after Joey Cooke's name was called, Coach Potter said, "Daniel Dodd."

Danny let out a yell.

Joey jumped up to give Danny a high-five. "The Flyers!" cried Danny.

14

Walter had a sick feeling in his stomach as Coach Potter read through the rest of the players' names. His name was not called.

"That's it," said Coach Potter. He looked up from his clipboard. "Your team coaches will give you your positions later. You all did well. I've seen a lot of talent here today. It's going to be a great season for the Rockville League. Play hard and have fun!"

Walter watched everyone join their teams. He felt numb. Danny was surrounded by his new teammates. Walter walked over to him.

"The coach didn't call me." Walter dug the toe of his sneaker into the dirt. "You said I could fill in."

Danny looked at Walter. "I said, *maybe,* Walter. You knew you couldn't play on a fourth-grade team." The Flyers were all heading over to the Mickey Mantle diamond for their first team practice. Danny ran to catch up.

Walter wandered into the outfield of Mickey Mantle. He squashed every dandelion in his path.

"Hey, watch out!" A kid trying to catch a fly ball bumped right into Walter. They both tumbled to the ground. "We're playing a game here!"

"Go jump in a lake!" said Walter. He wished he had thought of something better to say. But it was hard to think on the worst day of his life.

Walter turned to get off the field. He knew when he wasn't wanted.

Then Walter heard it—his favorite sound.

Crack! It was the sound of a solid hit.

Walter turned to see a baseball headed for second base. Then it cut right through the baseman's legs and kept going.

Without thinking, Walter knelt down, scooped up the ball, and threw it in to the pitcher.

"Way to go!" An outfielder ran up to Walter and slapped him on the back.

Had Coach Potter seen his great play? Walter looked toward the dugout. The coach was signaling for him to come in. His wish had come true! He was going to get on the team. Coach Potter would realize there had been some mistake. Walter was sure of it.

Walter ran in to the dugout.

"Nice save," said Coach Potter.

"Thanks." Walter's heart beat fast as he looked around the diamond.

"How old are you, son?"

"Eight and three-quarters," Walter said. When he saw Coach Potter's face he wished he had said "almost nine."

"I'm sorry, son. That's too young for this team. Tryouts for your age group were last week and those teams are filled up now. Come on out next year and I know you'll make it."

"Okay, Coach," Walter said. He felt terrible. He looked over at Danny on first base. Danny had just tagged a runner out. *I hate him,* thought Walter. But he knew he didn't mean it.

"Hey, Walter!" A boy in the bleachers was waving a sheet of paper in the air. It was Tony Pappas. Last month he'd broken his leg and his leg was in a cast. All he ever did was sit around drawing pictures.

He's probably the only person in Rockville who's worse off than me, thought Water. He waved half-heartedly at Tony and cut across the park.

CHAPTER THREE

Walter to Walter

"You should've seen me, Dad." Danny swung an imaginary bat across the dinner table. Mr. Dodd pretended to dodge the ball.

"He wasn't so great,"mumbled Walter.

Danny had been talking about his team's first practice all night. Every time Walter looked at Danny's Flyers' cap he felt angry.

"Sounds like quite a team," said Grandpa Walt. Walter's grandfather had dinner with them every Friday night.

Grandpa Walt put a hand on Walter's

shoulder. "Maybe we should practice so you'll be ready for the Rockville League next year."

"Who cares?" said Walter, mashing down his peas. How could Grandpa Walt understand? He had played semiprofessional baseball in the minor leagues as a young man.

"Don't play with your food, Walter," said Mrs. Dodd.

Walter took his plate out to the kitchen. He was sick of his family. They had no idea how terrible it felt to be left out of the league.

Walter's mother yelled to him through the kitchen door. "Don't forget to take out the garbage!"

Walter separated the garbage for recycling. Then he dragged the heavy trash can outside. He pulled it down the driveway to the street. He gave the garbage can a kick, pulled up his jeans, and looked at his socks. "Some lucky socks you turned out to be."

Walter sat down and took off his sneakers. Then he peeled off the socks that were supposed to bring good luck on the baseball field. He had taken them from Danny's drawer over a month ago. Walter balled them up and threw them in the trash.

"I don't care if you were Danny's," he said, closing the lid. "Your luck stinks and so do you!"

He heard the front door open and bang shut. Grandpa Walt walked across the lawn. "Isn't April a little early to go barefoot?"

Walter slipped on his sneakers. They felt cold against his skin.

"How about going for a drive?" Grandpa Walt tossed his car keys in the air and caught them.

Walter loved to go places with his grandfather. Grandpa Walt was a retired bus driver. He was happiest behind the wheel.

"Sorry, Grandpa. I have to put together my science project. It's a mobile of the solar system."

"Mm-m-m-m." Grandpa Walt stroked his chin thoughtfully. "Got your fluorescent paint yet?"

Walter shook his head. "What's that?"

"It'll light up your planets so they glow in the dark." He walked over to the driveway and opened the door to his car. "I've got some over at my place. Grab your planets and let's get this show on the road."

Walter ran inside to get his backpack and tell his mother where he was going. Then they were on their way. As soon as they drove into downtown Rockville, Grandpa Walt pulled into the drive-in ice cream place.

"First things first," he said, and got them two large chocolate ice cream cones. Grandpa Walt finished his cone first. "Let's talk Walter to Walter," he said. "You start."

Walter knew he meant just the two of them, man to man. Walter didn't know how to begin. It was hard talking about your feelings. He licked his cone until he was ready.

"Everyone on Danny's team is nine or ten," he started. "They don't want me because I'm eight." Walter felt good finally telling someone. "He's already called Danny the

23

Driver. I'll never get a good nickname out of Walter."

He was afraid Grandpa Walt might be mad. It was his name, too. But Grandpa Walt just nodded. "Go on."

"Coach Potter says all the teams for my age are full." Walter felt like crying so he took a big bite of ice cream.

Grandpa Walt seemed to understand. "What do you say we work on your project at my place?"

Walter quickly nodded. He loved visiting Grandpa Walt's apartment. It was right over Chung's Restaurant. The rooms always smelled like egg foo yung, Walter's personal favorite.

Grandpa Walt unlocked his apartment door and Walter headed straight for the steering wheel mounted above the fireplace. It was from the first bus Grandpa Walt ever drove. Walter reached up and gave it a spin.

Walter and Grandpa Walt spread newspaper over the floor. Then Walter got out his planets. Nine white balls. The smallest was

Pluto. The biggest was Jupiter. Walter wasn't sure yet about the others.

"Where's the sun?" asked Grandpa Walt.

"I forgot it," said Walter.

"No problem." Grandpa Walt took an orange from a bowl of fruit. "Here's your sun," he said.

Walter smiled. It was perfect.

Grandpa Walt stirred the paint. Then he handed a brush to Walter. "You paint the first one."

Walter chose a medium-sized planet. It had an *E* on it, for Earth.

He covered it with bright yellow paint. His favorite color.

"Magic time," said Grandpa Walt. He switched off all the lights.

"Wow!" Walter couldn't believe his eyes. The small yellow ball glowed like a lightbulb in the dark.

Grandpa Walt switched the lights back on and Walter watched the planet turn back into an ordinary ball in his hand.

"How many planets are there in this solar system of yours?" asked Grandpa Walt.

That was easy. "Nine," said Walter.

Then Grandpa Walt asked a strange question. "How many players do you need on a baseball team?"

"You know, Grandpa."

He asked again. "How many?"

"Nine."

"Just like the planets." Then Grandpa Walt started searching through his desk for something. He pulled out an old, yellowed piece of newspaper. He held it in front of Walter. It read:

THE NORTH DAKOTA NINE
WIN AGAIN

"My old team in the minors," said Grandpa Walt. "In those days a lot of guys came to the league with their own teams. As long as you had nine players and a coach they had to let you in." He held up the ball Walter had painted. "One down. Eight to go. We'd better get busy."

Walter grabbed a planet and started painting.

On the way home Grandpa Walt drove past Diamond Park. Planets and players kept going through Walter's mind. He looked out the window at the field where tryouts had been. "I've never heard of anyone who joined the league with their own team," he said quietly.

His grandfather shrugged. "No law against it. You just need nine."

Grandpa Walt's words went through Walter's head. *You just need nine. I'm one,* thought Walter. *That leaves eight.*

They turned onto Walter's street. "Elm Street and River Road," Grandpa Walt announced. He sounded like a real city bus driver. "Last stop, the Dodd home." He pulled up in front of Walter's house. " 'Night, sport," he said.

Walter didn't move. He looked at Grandpa Walt. He had made up his mind. "Know where I can find a good coach?" he said with a smile.

Grandpa Walt smiled back. "You're looking at him. Official coach *and* driver." He gave Walter a hug. "You just let me know when you've got a team, and I'll see Coach Potter about getting the team in the league. Deal?"

"Deal," said Walter and climbed out of the car. His backpack felt lighter without the planets inside. He had left the mobile at Grandpa Walt's to finish later.

Nine planets, nine players, thought Walter, jogging across the lawn. It wasn't going to be easy getting together a whole team by himself. He could use all the luck he could get.

Walter stopped on the doorstep. Maybe he'd give Danny's socks a second chance.

Walter set down his backpack and ran back down to the street. He lifted the trash-can lid and dug through soup cans and milk cartons. Under a mountain of banana peels he saw a small spot of purple. He pulled out the soggy socks.

Walter needed those socks. And he needed their luck now more than ever.

CHAPTER FOUR

Baseball Fever

On Saturday morning Walter woke up and looked in the mirror.

He saw a long pink line across his cheek. He had slept on his mitt and the leather stitches left a mark that looked like a scar. He looked tough.

Walter punched his mitt. He *felt* tough. Today he was going to find his own baseball team.

First things first. He dialed the Laskys' telephone number. Mike answered.

"Lasky residence."

Walter tried hard not to laugh. Mike's mom made him answer the phone that way. Walter got right down to business.

"It's Walter. I'm starting a baseball team. Want to join?"

Mike chewed his gum for a minute. "I guess so. Who else is on the team?"

"Just me," said Walter. "See you in five."

Two down, seven to go. Walter headed to the kitchen for breakfast. He was going to need all the energy he could get.

Walter spooned Mrs. Olsen's Oat Bran into his mouth as he studied the picture on the back of the cereal box. An official Babe Ruth wristwatch for twelve box tops. He tore off the box top and stuffed it in his pocket. Just two more and it was his.

"Morning, sports fans." Danny sat down next to Walter. He was wearing pajamas *and* his new Flyers' cap. "What's up, little Walt?"

"Nothing *you* would care about," Walter said into his cereal. "I'm just starting my *own* team, that's all."

31

"All *right,* squirt," Danny said. He leaned over to mess up Walter's hair, but Walter was already at the kitchen door. He raced outside, hopped on his bike, and headed for the Laskys'.

Walter found Mike helping his dad paint their front door. The Laskys' shared a house with another family. Their duplex had two front doors. One was red. The Laskys' was blue.

"Hi, Mr. Lasky." Walter had never seen Mike's father out of uniform. He was a police officer.

Mr. Lasky waved his paintbrush in the air. "Hello there, Mr. Dodd." He was the only person who ever called Walter "Mr. Dodd." It made Walter feel grown-up.

Walter walked his bike over to Mike. "Ready to go?"

"I can't." Mike was covered with blue paint.

Mr. Lasky lifted Mike's paintbrush out of his hand. "I'll finish up here. You two go on and find yourselves a team."

32

"Thanks, Dad." Mike went to the garage to get his bike.

One minute later Mike followed Walter toward town. They took the shortcut across Melrose Lane.

"Hey, look." Mike pointed up ahead. Melissa Nichols was galloping across her front lawn. She jumped over a small fence. Katie Kessler followed behind her. Plastic horses lined the sidewalk in front of Melissa's house.

Mike smiled at Walter and then looked at the horses. He wondered if Walter was thinking the same thing he was. They both headed for Melissa's prized horse collection.

Just as Walter's front tire was about to hit the first horse Melissa screamed. "Stop! Stop!" She lunged for the horse.

Walter swerved off the sidewalk to miss her. He landed in a row of thorny bushes. Mike screeched to a stop behind him.

"Ouch," said Walter, untangling himself. Mike helped him out of the bushes. Walter looked at his arm. There was a long red

scratch near his elbow. "I'm wounded," he said, holding it up.

"Gross," said Mike, looking away. "Good thing it's not your throwing arm."

"Serves you right," said Melissa, cradling her horse.

"Leaving toys on the sidewalk is against the law," said Mike. "My Dad could arrest you for that."

"But you were trying to run them over," said Melissa. "That must be against the law, too."

Melissa turned to Katie. "Guard my horses." She narrowed her eyes at Walter. "You'd better not touch Misty," she warned and went inside.

When she came out she had a bottle of iodine and some adhesive bandages. The iodine burned. Walter clenched his teeth. He looked down at his arm. The bandage had little ponies on it. Each one was a different color.

"You're lucky I'm not a doctor yet," said Melissa. "I'd charge you."

"Thanks," said Walter. He didn't know what else to say.

Melissa and Katie started picking up the horses on the sidewalk.

"Let's go," Mike said to Walter. "We'll never get a team together."

"What kind of team?" asked Katie.

"Nothing *you* can be on," Mike said with a laugh.

"I'm not so sure," said Walter. Having girls on the team might be the answer to his problem. Most of the boys were already in the league. Besides, Melissa was the best pitcher in the third grade. And Katie was pretty good at bat.

"A baseball team," said Walter. "Want to join?"

Mike's mouth dropped open. "I thought this was going to be all guys."

"Our first practice game is next week," said Walter.

"But they're *girls*," Mike whispered.

36

"I know, stupid," said Walter. "We don't have a choice. Besides, they're good players."

"So what's it going to be?" Walter asked.

"Okay," said Melissa. "We'll join."

Four down, five to go, thought Walter.

"On one condition," Melissa added. "I get to be pitcher. And Katie gets to be clean-up batter."

"No way!" said Mike.

"Take it or leave it." Melissa put her hands on her hips. Katie crossed her arms.

"It's up to the coach," said Walter. "I'll see what I can do."

They left the girls and headed for downtown Rockville. Walter bicycled next to Mike. "Only five more players to go," he said.

"This is hard work," Mike said. "I need a soda."

"Good idea," said Walter. "Let's stop at Klugman's."

They parked their bikes in front of Klugman's Drugstore.

"Back in a flash," said Walter.

He walked to the cooler at the back of the store and took the last two cans of orange soda.

There was a long line at the cash register. A tall skinny boy was standing at the end holding a box of Kleenex. It was Felix Smith. He and Walter had gym class together.

Walter tapped Felix on the shoulder.

Felix turned around. His nose was red and his eyes were watery. "Oh, hi, Walter."

"You don't look so hot," said Walter.

Felix tore open the box of Kleenex and pulled out a tissue. "Happens every spring," he said. "It's my . . . a-a-a-ah-choo!" He blew his nose. ". . . allergies."

"Too bad," said Walter. "I'll bet regular exercise would help. A sport, maybe. Something like baseball."

Felix dabbed his nose with a tissue. "Think so?"

Walter nodded. "Actually I'm getting a

team together for the Rockville League. Want to join?" he asked casually.

By the time Walter paid for the sodas, Felix couldn't wait for their first practice.

Walter walked by the candy section on the way out. Otis Hooper was loading up on candy bars.

Otis was the biggest kid in the third grade. He was also the oldest. Otis had flunked last year. He was supposed to be in Danny's class. Walter hadn't noticed Otis at tryouts.

Player number six, thought Walter. "Hi, Otis."

"Hi." Otis held up a handful of candy bars. "Three for a dollar," he said.

Walter thought fast. "You know, the more calories you work off playing baseball, the more candy you can eat."

"Could I be catcher?" Otis asked.

"Sure," said Walter.

"Okay. Count me in."

By the time Walter got outside the sodas were warm. Mike was talking to a girl in a pink leotard and white tights. It was Christy Chung.

"Hi, Christy," said Walter. He turned to Mike. "I got us two more players."

"Three," said Christy. She flipped her long black hair over one shoulder. "Mike just asked me to join."

"*Another* girl!" Walter said. "Are you sure it's okay?" he added with a smile. Mike hadn't wanted any girls on the team, but Walter knew Mike liked Christy.

Mike shrugged and blushed deep pink. He smiled at Christy.

Walter counted off all the players on his fingers. Seven. "We need two more," he said.

"How about Billy Baskin?" said Christy. "He's a real slugger. I saw him skateboarding at Roosevelt on my way here from ballet class."

Walter and Mike finished their sodas and headed straight over to school. They found Billy skateboarding in the empty parking lot.

40

The three boys spent most of the afternoon practicing their freestyle tricks. Before they knew it, it was getting dark and Billy was the newest member of their team.

Mike checked his watch. "I've got to get home."

"But we need one more player," said Walter.

"We've got time." Mike turned his bike toward home and pushed off. "Later, terminator!"

Walter pedaled in the opposite direction. "In a while, juvenile!" He hoped Mike was right. Opening-day games were only two weeks away.

When Walter got home Danny was watching TV in his Flyers' uniform. "A *giiiiirrl* called you," Danny said. He grabbed a pillow from the couch and pretended to hug it. He made loud kissing noises.

"Very funny," said Walter and escaped to

the kitchen. Mrs. Dodd was making dinner. Saturday was spaghetti night.

"A girl named Melissa called," she said. "I left her number on the refrigerator."

Walter grabbed the number, went into the den and dialed the number.

Melissa got right to the point. "Mom says I have to watch out for my little sister after school."

"So what?" said Walter.

"I can't play on your team unless you let Jenny play, too."

"What position does she play?"

"She's never actually played baseball. But she's good at jumping rope," Melissa said slowly. "She's only a year younger than I am, and she's very athletic."

"Forget it!" Walter started to hang up.

"Without Jenny you'll never get your team together," Melissa said.

Walter groaned. She was right. "Okay," he said. "She's in."

Before bedtime Walter began spring

training. He started with twenty sit-ups on the bedroom floor. Now that he had a team he had to set an example.

He looked at Danny's uniform lying on his bed. It was caked with dirt. Winning dirt. The Flyers had won a practice game today.

Walter touched the edge of one sleeve.

Suddenly Danny appeared at the door. He let out a long and loud burp. Walter thought it sounded wonderful. He swallowed some air and tried. A small gurgling noise rose from his throat.

"Give it up," said Danny. He stepped over Walter and opened a drawer. "Hey, have you been messing around in my stuff again?"

"No."

Walter rolled over and did five quick push-ups so Danny wouldn't see his face. He had wanted to try the uniform on.

"I'm beat," said Danny, collapsing in bed. "I've got a game in the morning."

"You're not the only one," said Walter.

"I've got my own team now. We're going to sign up with the league on Monday."

"You did it!" Danny lifted his head from the pillow. "How many players do you have?"

"Nine."

Danny sat up in bed. "And a coach?"

"The best," said Walter. "Grandpa Walt."

Danny nodded his approval. "I'm impressed, little Walt." He leaned over the bed. "Who's your sponsor?"

"Sponsor?"

"You know," said Danny. "They buy the team uniforms and stuff. You can't be in the league without one."

"I know that," said Walter, crawling into bed. "We'll get one," he added as he turned out the light. But he wasn't exactly sure how they were going to do it.

CHAPTER FIVE

The Never Sink Nine

On Sunday, Walter parked his bike outside Chung's Restaurant. He had swiped Danny's sweatshirt that morning and the sleeves hung down over his hands. He pushed them up and went inside.

"Over here!" Grandpa Walt waved to him. He was sitting in a booth with Mike, Melissa, Melissa's sister Jenny, and Christy Chung. Christy's parents owned the restaurant right below Grandpa Walt's apartment.

"You're late," said Melissa.

"Let's get down to business," said Grandpa

Walt. "We have to find a sponsor and we don't have much time. Any suggestions?"

"We could ask all the stores in town," said Melissa.

"We could split up and take different sides of the street," added Walter. "That way we could save time."

"Now you're thinking like a team," said Grandpa Walt.

They agreed to meet back at the restaurant at three o'clock. Mr. Chung treated them all to chicken and snow peas before they left.

Walter and Mike were supposed to cover Sherman Avenue. On the street were Hazel's Bridal Boutique, the Book Nook, medical offices, and a pet shop.

Animal World was their first stop. Walter and Mike stood outside the pet shop rehearsing their sales pitch.

"Think they'll go for it?" asked Mike.

"Sure," said Walter. "My dad sells cars and he says all you gotta do is smile."

Walter opened the door. "Can I help you?" A woman stood behind the counter.

An ugly brown dog waddled out from behind the counter. He sniffed Walter's purple socks. Walter pushed him away and stepped forward.

"I'm Walter P. Dodd." He stopped and gave her his biggest smile. "My baseball team is trying to get into the Rockville League. But we need a sponsor. Can you help us?"

"Sorry," said the woman. "I'm already sponsoring my son's team." She nodded toward a pudgy boy cleaning a cat box. He was wearing a baseball uniform. BRONCO DOGS was printed across the back of his shirt.

"Lenny," said the woman, "these boys need a sponsor. Do you have any ideas?"

The boy turned around. WE'RE TOUGH was printed across the front of his shirt. "Yeah," he said, with a sneer. "Give up. All the good stores are taken."

"Ha, ha," said Walter. "Very funny."

"Yeah," said Mike and followed his friend out the door.

By two-thirty Walter and Mike were ready to quit. They had been to eight stores and all of them had said no.

Mike sat down on the curb and pulled out a fresh piece of gum. "I'm tired of begging," he said. "We've hit every store in sight."

"Except this one," said Walter.

The store window in front of them read Never Sink Plumbers, Inc. It had a little picture of a dripping faucet. Underneath it said, We Make Your Home Run.

Walter and Mike entered the tiny store. The walls were covered with toilet seats in bright colors. Rubber plungers hung down from the ceiling.

A man in overalls came out from the back. "What can I do to help you boys?" he asked.

"We need a sponsor," said Walter. He had no time for his speech.

"For our baseball team," added Mike.

The man hooked his thumbs under his

overall straps and rocked back and forth on his heels.

"I'll do it," he said.

"What?" Walter couldn't believe his ears.

"I said I'll sponsor your team." The man looked straight into his eyes. "On one condition."

"*Anything,*" said Walter.

"That you make my son an honorary member. You see he can't play this season, but he loves the game."

"No problem," Mike said quickly.

The man shouted toward a back room. "Tony!"

A boy with a broken leg came hobbling out on crutches. He had a drawing pencil stuck behind one ear.

It was Tony Pappas!

"Hi, Tony," said Mike. He jabbed Walter in the side.

Walter forced a smile. "Welcome to the team."

CHAPTER SIX

The Never Stink Nine

The Never Sink Nine had their first team practice on Monday after school. It was on the Willie Mays diamond.

Since Tony couldn't play, Grandpa Walt let him take roll call. Everyone was there.

"We're off to a good start," said Grandpa Walt. He was wearing a sweatshirt with COACH written across the front.

"Walter promised I could be pitcher," said Melissa.

"He said I could be catcher," added Otis.

"First let's see how everyone does out on

51

the field," said Grandpa Walt. "I'm going to shag some flys. You try to catch them."

All the players raced for their favorite positions. Walter dashed for second base. Mike took shortstop next to Walter.

Grandpa Walt tossed a ball in the air and took a swing.

Crack!

The ball sailed up over Walt's head deep into the outfield.

"Wow!" said Mike.

Walter felt proud. He couldn't believe his own grandfather was that strong. He watched the ball head straight for Felix in left field.

"Get it, Felix!" everyone shouted.

Felix closed his eyes and covered his head. He started running *away* from the ball.

Thud.

The ball hit the ground. When it finally rolled to a stop, Felix opened his eyes. "It was gonna hit me," he said.

Walter looked at Mike and shook his head.

The next ball was a line drive through the infield. It was headed in Walter's direction.

"I've got it!" said Walter.

"It's mine!" said Mike.

Walter and Mike rushed for the ball at the same time. They crashed into each other.

Walter was beginning to wonder if this team was such a good idea after all. He heard someone shouting.

"It's green! I saw it!" Jenny was hopping up and down in right field.

"Snake!" yelled Christy, running for the dugout. "Snake!"

"That's ridiculous," said Walter. He looked down in the grass by his feet. "There aren't any snakes out here." Then he thought he saw something move. Something slimy and slithery and green!

"Wait for me!" Walter jumped and ran after them.

Everyone huddled together in the dugout.

"I saw it!" said Jenny. "It hissed!"

Walter watched his grandfather bravely walk out into the field. "What if it's poisonous?" he said softly.

"Don't worry." Melissa was hugging her backpack filled with horses. "If it's a rattler I know what to do. I saw a cowboy get bit by one on TV."

Grandpa Walt held something up over his head. Something long and slithery.

It was a jump rope. Long and green.

"Some snake," said Walter.

Melissa put an arm around Jenny. "You ran just as fast as she did, Walter."

Walter punched his mitt. He didn't know what to say.

By the time the snake scare was over, it was getting dark.

"Baseball skills aren't learned in one day," said Grandpa Walt. "You all did a good job. You tried your best. Now I have some good news. Our sponsor put a rush order on our uniforms and they should arrive before our first practice game."

55

"What color are they?" asked Melissa.

"A very special color for a special team," said Grandpa Walt. "Light blue and white."

"You mean *baby* blue," said Mike.

All the boys groaned. Walter knew the good colors had already been taken by the other teams in the league.

"*Sky* blue," said Grandpa Walt. "That's where we're going to be hitting all our balls."

"When's our first game?" Walter was almost afraid to ask.

"Thursday," said Grandpa Walt. "A practice game against the Bronco Dogs."

Walter jabbed Mike in the arm. "The creep from Animal World," he whispered.

"Remember," said Grandpa Walt, "whether we win or lose, we're all winners on this team. Right?"

"Right," everyone answered. But they didn't sound as if they believed it.

"We stink," said Walter, heading for the car.

"Yeah, we're the Never Stink Nine," Mike said, right behind him.

Everyone loaded into Grandpa Walt's station wagon.

The only member of the Never Sink Nine who seemed happy was Tony Pappas. "Wanna see my pictures?" he said, passing them around.

"Heh, this one is funny," said Melissa. She showed it to Katie and they burst out laughing. She shoved it in Walter's lap.

It was a drawing of Walter bumping into Mike and the ball going between their legs.

"Can I keep this one?" Walter asked Tony.

"Sure," said Tony.

Walter folded it up and stuffed it in his pocket. If anyone at school saw it, he'd never live it down.

"Hey, I can actually breathe in here," said Melissa. "Walter must not be wearing his stinko socks."

Walter looked down at his ankles. That was

it! He had forgotten to wear his lucky socks. He borrowed a pencil from Tony and wrote a note to himself.

thursday, practice game with b.dogs.
DON'T FORGET—LUCKY SOCKS!!!!!!

CHAPTER SEVEN

The Bronco Dogs Game

It was the day of the game. Right after lunch the players had been allowed to change into their uniforms. Walter couldn't wait to get his new uniform dirty.

He looked up at the blackboard. Mrs. Howard had written Quiet Hour. He didn't think he could be quiet much longer.

Melissa turned around in her seat. Never Sink Nine was printed across her shirt in light blue letters.

Melissa sniffed the air. "P.U.!" she said,

pinching her nose. "Don't you ever wash those things?" She looked at his socks with disgust.

"No, dummy," he said, rubbing his socks together. "It'd wash the luck out."

"Misty's good luck," said Melissa, patting the backpack under her chair. "And I wash her all the time."

"I hear talking." Mrs. Howard's voice came from the front of the room.

Melissa quickly turned around.

Just then the school bell rang. Everyone started gathering their things to go. Walter, Melissa, and Mike ran down the hall together. The team had agreed to meet outside school and walk to Diamond Park together.

Grandpa Walt was waiting for them at the Babe Ruth diamond. He took a photo of the team in front of the dugout. Everyone looked great in their new uniforms, even Tony. He had one pants leg split up the side to make room for his cast.

"You look like a real major league team in

those uniforms," said Grandpa Walt. "Think you can play like one?"

No one answered. They were busy watching the Bronco Dogs warm up on the field.

"*They* look like major leaguers," said Mike.

"Yeah," agreed Walter. "We've only had two practices. They've been practicing much longer."

Even their team mascot looked tough. Lenny's dog was chasing after the ball in a T-shirt with WE'RE TOUGH on the side.

"No excuses," said Grandpa Walt. "As long as we've got team spirit, we have a good chance."

The game didn't get off to a good start. By the fourth inning the Bronco Dogs were ahead two to zero. And Walter hadn't gotten one hit.

It was Melissa's turn at bat.

"Easy out!" shouted the Bronco Dogs' pitcher. It was Lenny, the boy from the pet store.

Melissa looked nervous. She took three

quick swings and struck out. She took her place next to Walter on the bench. "The sun was in my eyes," she said.

Walter swallowed. He hoped he did better. It was his turn next.

He stepped into the batter's box. He gripped the bat so tight his knuckles turned white. He wasn't going to swing until he was good and ready.

He let three balls go by.

"Ball four!" said the umpire as the last ball zipped by. "Take your base!"

Walter jogged to first base. At least he was in the game.

Grandpa Walt gave him a thumbs-up sign. "Good eye!"

Billy Baskin was up next. He was their best hitter. Unfortunately the Bronco Dogs had caught every one of his fly balls.

Crack!

Billy hit a solid hit to the outfield!

"Run!" shouted Grandpa Walt.

"Go!" screamed Walter's teammates.

Walter dashed to second base. The Bronco Dogs outfielder had touched the ball with the tip of his mitt and the ball bounced to the ground.

Walter ran for third base. He held his breath and didn't look back until he crossed home plate. Billy Baskin was right behind him. They had gotten two runs.

The score was tied two to two!

The Bronco Dogs looked mad. *Really* mad.

Billy Baskin managed to hit another home run. By the last inning the score was three to two in The Never Sink Nine's favor. The Bronco Dogs were up at bat. They had two outs. The bases were loaded. If the Bronco Dogs got a base hit, they'd win the game.

Lenny stepped up to home plate. He had made a hit each time he was up to bat. He took a couple of practice swings and waited for Melissa's pitch.

Melissa dug her feet in the mound. She wound up and threw her fastball.

Crack!

Lenny hit a long fly ball.

Walter looked up. He could barely see the ball. Lenny and the others started trotting around the bases.

The Bronco Dogs were cheering as if they had already won.

But Walter kept his eye on the ball. He wasn't going to give up now. He ran into the outfield as fast as he could. He knew the ball was coming down any second. But where? He backed up. He ran forward. The sun was in his eyes. Walter lifted his mitt.

Thunk!

The ball hit the center of his mitt.

"Out!" shouted the umpire.

The Never Sink Nine threw their mitts into the air and raced over to meet Walter on the field. Mike ran right into Walter. They crashed to the ground, laughing.

The final score was three to two. The Never Sink Nine had won its first game!

After all the equipment was put away, Walter went back to the dugout. He wanted to take off his lucky socks.

"From now on I'm just wearing you guys at games." Walter laid the lucky socks down on the bench. They were much to valuable to wear off the field.

"Come on!" yelled Mike. Everyone was piling into Grandpa Walt's station wagon. "Coach is taking us to the Pizza Palace!"

Just then the Bronco Dogs' mascot came sniffing around the dugout. "Get out of here," said Walter. As he turned to pick up his mitt the bulldog grabbed the socks and ran out to home plate.

"Hey, give me those!" shouted Walter, running after him. He pulled on the socks with all his might. The dog pulled back. The socks stretched like taffy between them. Then they tore in half.

Walter stood still. He blinked hard to hold back the tears. He looked down at the tiny purple scrap in his hand.

Grandpa Walt drove up and honked the horn.

"Hurry up!" Mike pulled Walter into the car. "We're hungry!"

At the Pizza Palace Grandpa Walt ordered three extra-large pepperoni pizzas. But Walter didn't feel like eating.

After everyone had finished, Tony Pappas passed around his drawings of the game. Some of them were really good. Then the team took turns signing his cast. Tony wanted Walter to sign his name first. "Since you made the winning catch," he said.

By the time Grandpa Walt drove everyone home it was nearly dark outside.

Mike was the last one to be dropped off. He grabbed his mitt and jumped out of the car. "See you later, alligator!"

Walter just waved good-bye as they drove off. Then he climbed into the front seat with Grandpa Walt.

Something was rolling around on the car

floor. It was his solar system mobile. He picked it up and rested it on his lap. Grandpa Walt had hung all the planets from a wire clothes hanger.

"Thanks," said Walter. "Just in time to hand in tomorrow."

Grandpa Walt nodded. When they came to a stop sign he turned to Walter. "Not bad for our first game, eh, Champ?"

"Yeah," said Walter. "But . . ." He didn't know how to explain. His lucky socks were gone.

Grandpa Walt took one hand off the steering wheel and reached across Walter. He pushed a button. The glove compartment sprang open. Nestled on top of roadmaps was a small package.

"For you," said Grandpa Walt. "Open it."

Walter didn't waste any time. He loved gifts. He ripped open the small soft package. Inside was a brand new pair of sky blue socks.

"Thought your old ones looked a little big," he said.

Walter kicked off his sneakers and pulled

68

on the new socks. They fit perfectly. They didn't sag around his ankles like Danny's had.

He leaned his head against Grandpa Walt's shoulder. "Do you believe in luck?" he asked.

Grandpa Walt shrugged. "You mean like beginner's luck?"

Walter nodded.

"Sure," he said, pulling out his lucky penny. Walter touched it. "A lot of baseball players do. But we'll have to find out if today was beginner's luck when we play the Drill Team. Opening-day game is the real test. We have a lot of work to do before then."

Walter looked at his socks. Was it luck that made him make that winning catch? He wouldn't know until the big opening-day game.

Grandpa Walt pulled up in front of Walter's house. "Last stop, the Dodd house," he said.

Walter leaned over and gave Grandpa Walt a long hug. Then he climbed out of the car.

"See you at practice, Slugger!" shouted Grandpa Walt.

Walter held the solar system out in front of him as he walked across the lawn. The glowing planets bobbed up and down in the dark. One of them hit a bush and all nine spun around. They were perfectly balanced.

He looked down at his new blue socks. *No one will know they're lucky,* he thought. *And I won't tell them—not even Danny.*

Walter threw his whole weight against the front door. "Watch out, Drill Team!" he said, bursting in. He let the door slam shut behind him.

ABOUT THE AUTHOR

GIBBS DAVIS was born in Milwaukee, Wisconsin, graduated from the University of California at Berkeley, and lives in New York City. Her first novel, *Maud Flies Solo,* is also a Bantam Skylark book. She has published *Swann Song,* a young adult novel, with Avon Books. *Walter's Lucky Socks* is the first book in The Never Sink Nine series for First Skylark.

ABOUT THE ILLUSTRATOR

GEORGE ULRICH was born in Morristown, New Jersey, and received his Bachelor of Fine Arts from Syracuse University. He has illustrated several Bantam Skylark books, including *Make Four Million Dollars by Next Thursday!* by Stephen Manes and *The Amazing Adventure of Me, Myself, and I* by Jovial Bob Stine. He lives in Marblehead, Massachusetts, with his wife and two sons.

SKYLARK BOOKS
can be *your* special friends

☐ 15615 **THE WHITE STALLION** by Elizabeth Shub.
$2.75 ($3.25 in Canada) Long ago, a proud white
stallion roamed the plains of Texas. Cowboys said
he was the greatest horse that ever lived. Gretchen
discovers, in a scary, exciting adventure, that they
were right.

☐ 15777 **JACK GALAXY, SPACE COP**
by Robert Kraus. $2.75 ($3.25 in Canada)
Jack zooms through the universe fighting space
crime with his best friend Sally and Jojo the space
dog. Giant hamburgers are taking over the world
and only Jack & his friends can save the day!

☐ 15711 **BUMPS IN THE NIGHT** by Harry Allard.
$2.50 ($2.95 in Canada) Dudley the Stork finds out
his new house is haunted and is determined to find
out just who the ghost is.

Buy them wherever paperback books are sold—or order below.

Wild and crazy adventures from
<u>Stephen Manes!</u>

☐ **BE A PERFECT PERSON IN**
JUST THREE DAYS!   15580-6 $2.95

Milo Crinkley tries to follow the loony instructions on being
perfect, found in a library book. But who ever heard of wearing
a stalk of broccoli around your neck for twenty-four hours? And
that's only the first day...

☐ **IT'S NEW! IT'S IMPROVED!**
IT'S TERRIBLE!   15682-9 $2.75

The TV commercials say the shoes that basketball star Ralph
"Helicopter" Jones wears are "New! IMPROVED! Amazing!
NEAT!" Arnold Schlemp just has to have them. At least until
the commercial steps out of his TV set and into his life!

☐ **CHICKEN TREK**   15716-7 $2.75

Oscar Noodleman spends his summer vacation entering the
"Chicken in the Bag" contest and eating 211 chicken meals at
restaurants across America! But Oscar's not the only one after
the $99,999.99 prize. Join the Chicken Trek!

Buy them at your local bookstore or use this page to order:

CHOOSE YOUR OWN ADVENTURE®

SKYLARK EDITIONS

☐	15744	**Circus #1**	$2.50
☐	15679	**Haunted House #2**	$2.50
☐	15680	**Green Slime #6**	$2.50
☐	15562	**Summer Camp #18**	$2.50
☐	15732	**Haunted Harbor #33**	$2.50
☐	15453	**Haunted Halloween Party #37**	$2.50
☐	15492	**The Great Easter Adventure #40**	$2.50
☐	15742	**The Movie Mystery #41**	$2.50
☐	15709	**Home in Time for Christmas #43**	$2.50
☐	15612	**Day With Dinosaurs #46**	$2.50
☐	15672	**Spooky Thanksgiving #47**	$2.50
☐	15685	**You Are Invisible #48**	$2.50
☐	15696	**Race of the Year #49**	$2.75
☐	15762	**Stranded! #50**	$2.75
☐	15776	**You Can Make a Difference: The Story of Martin Luther King, Jr.**	$2.50